VERONICA'S CHALLENGE

DOTTI HENDERSON

VERONICA'S
CHALLENGE

VERONICA'S CHALLENGE

DOTTI HENDERSON

ARPress
45 Dan Road Suite 5
Canton MA 02021

Hotline: 1(800) 220-7660
Fax: 1(855) 752-6001

Ordering Information:
Quantity sales. Special discounts are available on quantity purchases by corporations, associations, and others. For details, contact the publisher at the address above.

Printed in the United States of America.

ISBN-13:   Paperback   979-8-89389-681-7
            eBook   979-8-89389-682-4

Library of Congress Control Number: 2024923899

eronica was packing for her trip back home to New York. Her mother walked into the room.

"Are you going to have breakfast with us before you leave?" her mom asked.

"Sure, I will. I don't have to leave right away," Veronica said.

"I'm going to check to make sure I haven't forgotten anything," Veronica told her mother.

As Veronica was getting ready to go downstairs, she thought "It's nice to be here again. This house has good memories."

Veronica was a tall, slim girl, with blonde hair and blue eyes. She came downstairs and sat in the dining room.

"Something smells good," she told her mom.

Her mom brought out blueberry muffins, scrambled eggs, bacon, sausage, and toast.

"Your father will be right down," her mom said. "He's finishing shaving."

"Good morning, Ronnie. Did you sleep well?" her father asked. "I sure did," she told him.

"I'm sorry I can't go to the airport; I have to get to the bank," he told her.

"That's okay, Dad. I'm glad we had some time together," she told him. He kissed them both good-bye, then went out the door.

"When is Melissa coming home?" Veronica asked. "She will be home in a month," her mom replied.

"Yes, that's right. Her graduation is soon. I can't wait to see her," Veronica said.

"Let's finish these dishes. Then I'll take you to the airport," her mom told her.

Veronica brought her bags to the car. When she came back in, her mom had something for her.

"What's this?" Veronica asked.

"It's from your father," her mom said.

"It's beautiful, a diamond necklace. I love it," Veronica said.

"We better get going," her mother said.

As they were driving to the airport, Veronica's mom told her it was nice to have her home.

"I enjoyed the visit, Mom," Veronica replied.

"What time is Trevor picking you up?" her mom asked.

"He's sending James; he couldn't get away," Veronica told her mother. "Well, here we are," her mom said.

"Okay, Mom, I'll call you later," Veronica said. "Okay, dear, safe trip home now," her mom said.

It was about 1:30 when Veronica got to the New York airport. At first, she didn't see James the chauffeur. But then she spotted him. "There he is," she said as she waved to him.

"Good afternoon, Veronica," he said. "Hi, James," she replied.

When James opened the door, Trevor was in the limousine. "Surprise!" he said.

"It sure is a wonderful surprise," Veronica told him.

He kissed her and told James to drive to Veronica's apartment.

"I thought you would like to go home first and freshen up," he told her.

"Yes, good idea," she said.

"Where would you like to go to for lunch?" Trevor asked. "How about Sandy's on the Beach?" Veronica said. "Good choice," he agreed.

A few minutes later, they drove to Veronica's apartment.

"We won't be long too long, James," Trevor told him.

"That's quite all right, sir," he said.

"Let me check my messages, then wash my face, and fix my makeup," Veronica told Trevor.

"Take your time, honey. You look real good," he told her. "Have I told you how much I have missed you?" Trevor asked.

"What did you say, Trevor? I couldn't hear you," Veronica said.

"I'll tell you when you get done," he said.

"Okay, honey, what were you saying again?" she asked.

"I just wanted you to know how much I missed you and to tell you I love you," he told her.

Then he kissed her softly on the mouth.

"I love you, too, Trevor. I'm glad I'm home now," Veronica told him. "Let's get some lunch," he told her.

They had to wait 10 minutes but got a nice table by the restaurant's window and had a view of the beach.

The waiter came over. Trevor ordered two glasses of wine. "We'll order lunch in a few minutes," he told the waiter.

"It's nice to have a quiet lunch with you, Trevor. I'm glad we are here together," Veronica told him.

Trevor noticed the diamond necklace Veronica was wearing. "Did you buy that necklace in New Jersey?" he asked.

"No, my father gave it to me. Isn't it beautiful?" she told him. "Your father has good taste," said Trevor.

"My parents were wondering, when we take our vacation, if we would like to come there for a few days," Veronica asked.

"I was thinking we could go to the mountains," Trevor said.

"Sure, Trevor, I'll make up some excuse," Veronica told him.

The waiter came back and took their order. They ordered two turkey club sandwiches with lots of pickles.

It took about 20 minutes before the food was on the table.

"How about we drive to the park after lunch? We'll get some ice cream," Trevor said.

"Sure, sounds good," said Veronica.

It was 3:15 when they got to the park. It was a beautiful day with the temperature about 70 degrees.

They walked for a while, eating their ice cream and holding hands. "It's nice to have time alone with you," she told him.

"In a little while, I have to drop you off," he told Veronica. "I thought we had the whole afternoon together," she said.

"I have a meeting, but we are going to dinner tonight, to The Red Rose.

Wear your sexiest dress. I'll pick you up at 8:00.," he told her.

"Okay, Trevor, I'll be ready," she told him.

After they said good-bye, Veronica made some phone calls. She tried to call her sister Melissa, but the line was busy. A few minutes later her own phone rang.

"Hi, Ronnie. It's me, Melissa," her sister said.

"Hey, I just tried to call you," Veronica told her.

"How was your trip with Mom and Dad,?" Melissa asked.

"It went well. I wanted to know what you wanted for your graduation," Veronica said.

"Just you to be there, sis," Melissa told her.

"I wouldn't miss it for the world, baby sister," Veronica told her.

Veronica hung up the phone and began looking for a dress to wear for her dinner with Trevor.

She pulled out a maroon dress from the back of the closet. "I'm sure Trevor will like this one," she told herself.

Veronica jumped into the shower, washed her hair, and shaved her legs.

She dried off and slipped on her dress. "Not bad," she thought as she glanced in the mirror.

The doorbell rang as she was putting on her lipstick. She opened the door.

"Well, hello. You look beautiful, Veronica," Trevor told her. "Thank you, Trevor," she said and smiled.

They got into a limousine and were on their way to The Red Rose.

They got to the restaurant on time. The waiter seated them at a private table.

"This place is busy tonight," Veronica said.

The waiter came over and took their drink orders and told them he would return in a few minutes to take their dinner order.

The table had a shimmering candle and a red rose in the middle. The waiter returned with their drinks and asked to take their orders. "We will have the lobster dinner for two," Trevor told him.

"I was wondering if you wanted to go to the lake after dinner," Trevor said to Veronica.

"I'd love to," she said.

It wasn't long before the waiter brought their lobsters. They were huge. "Wow!" said Veronica.

"I know. Well, let's eat," Trevor said.

When they finished dinner, the waiter asked if they wanted dessert.

"Just the check please," Trevor told him.

They got into the limousine, and James drove them to the lake. "It's so beautiful and clear here," Veronica said.

"Let's take a walk," Trevor told her.

He took her hand and walked closer to the water. Trevor turned to Veronica. "You are so beautiful. I love you so much. We have been together for two years now. I have to ask you something," he said, then hesitated.

"What's wrong, Trevor?" she asked.

"Bear with me for a minute," Trevor said as he reached into his pocket and took out a small box.

"Veronica, this is for you. Will you marry me?" he asked nervously.

She paused for a moment, then replied, Yes, I will marry you, Trevor.

"I love you."

"I was so nervous," he told her.

He leaned over and kissed her lips.

"Do you know how happy this makes me?" Veronica asked.

"I'm very happy, too," Trevor told her.

"I wish we could spend the night together," Veronica said. "We will soon, baby. I promise," he told her.

They finally got to Veronica's apartment.

"Well, good night, my love," he said.

"Good night, honey," she said and kissed him.

When Veronica got in her apartment, she was so excited. She looked at her ring again.

"I have to tell someone; I'll call Marcie," she told herself.

She dialed Marcie's number. The phone rang twice.

"Hello," Marcie answered.

"Hi, Marcie. "It's me, Ronnie.""

"Hey, girl, how was your trip?" she asked.

"It was wonderful," Veronica replied.

"How's Trevor doing?" Marcie asked.

"Well, as a matter of fact, I have some news," Veronica told her.

"Tell me what's up, Ronnie," Marcie said.

"Well, Trevor and I went to The Red Rose for dinner tonight, and after that we went to the lake, and he asked me to marry him!" she exclaimed.

"Wow, Ronnie! That is so great," Marcie said excitedly.

"I know. Isn't it?" Veronica said.

"Well, we have to celebrate. It's not too late. I'll come by, and we can drink wine and talk, okay?" Marcie said.

"Sure," Veronica agreed.

"Okay, I'll be there in 20 minutes," Marcie told her.

"Oh, Marcie, can you pick up another bottle of wine?" Veronica asked.

"Will do," Marcie said.

In no time Marcie was at the door.

"C'mon in, my best friend," Veronica said.

They hugged each other.

"I brought two bottles of wine, white and rose," Marcie told her.

Veronica went into the kitchen to get two wine glasses.

"Why aren't you with Trevor tonight?" Marcie asked Veronica.

"He had to go home. He has to go out of town for a meeting. He'll be back Wednesday," Veronica told her.

"Well, it's girls' night tonight," Marcie said.

"Let's drink to us first, then to Trevor later," Marcie said.

They both laughed out loud.

"This wine is great, Marcie.

I'll have more please," Veronica said.

"Let's dance," Marcie said.

"I love to dance," Veronica said with a giggle.

They danced a few songs then sat on the couch.

"Don't tell me you are tired already, Ronnie?" Marcie asked.

"No, just taking a wine break," Veronica told her. "Sit with me for a minute."

"So, are you excited about your engagement, Ronnie?" Marcie asked.

"Yes, very, and I want you to be my maid of honor," Veronica told her.

"I would love to. I accept, Ronnie," Marcie said, and Veronica gave Marcie a hug.

"You really are my best friend," Veronica said to Marcie.

"I should be going soon," Marcie said.

"No, stay. The pizza will be here any minute," Veronica told her. "Let's find a movie to watch."

"I'll get us another glass of wine," Marcie said.

The doorbell rang.

"There's the pizza; I'll get it," Veronica said.

"Mmmm. Smells so good," Marcie told her.

"Will you stay over with me?" Veronica asked Marcie.

"Sure, if you want me to," Marcie said.

"We won't be able to do this when you are married," Marcie told her.

"Well, we have now anyway," Veronica said.

"Last piece. You want it?" Veronica asked.

"No, you finish it," Marcie told her.

"Well, I'm getting tired," Veronica told her.

"Me, too, I better get some sleep, too," Marcie said.

"I'll sleep on the couch."

"Okay, you're sure you'll be comfortable there?" Veronica asked.

"Yes, I will be," Marcie told her.

"Okay, see you in the morning," Veronica said.

"I'll just finish my wine," Marcie told her.

"Good night, Marcie."

"Good night, Ronnie."

Morning came. Veronica went into the kitchen. Marcie was on the couch.

Veronica made some coffee, and its smell woke Marcie up.

"Good morning, Marcie," Veronica said.

"Morning," Marcie said.

"Did you sleep well?" Veronica asked.

"I lay down here, and I was out," Marcie told her.

"I'll make breakfast," Veronica said.

"I should go," said Marcie.

"Why?" Veronica asked.

"I'll call you later, for lunch," Marcie told her.

"Okay," said Veronica.

Veronica hugged Marcie before she left.

"I wonder what that was about," Veronica thought to herself.

Veronica picked up the paper outside the door. She started to read it.

The phone rang. It was Trevor.

"Is this my bride to be?" he asked.

"It sure is," she answered.

"I wanted to call you before I left for my trip," he told her.

"Well, I'm glad you called, honey," she said. "Have a safe trip."

"Okay, I love you," he told her.

"I love you, too," she said.

After taking a shower, Veronica had to get to her job at the aquarium for practice for an afternoon show.

She got there fifteen minutes early. She wanted to see the dolphins, Wally and Wendy. Veronica walked into the training room. Sonny, one of the trainers, was there.

"Hi, Sonny," Veronica said.

"Hey, Ronnie, how are you doing today?" he asked.

"Very well, thanks," she replied.

"How are Wally and Wendy feeling today?" she asked.

"They seem to be in a very good mood today," he told her.

Veronica walked to the dolphin pool area. "Hello, Wally. Hello, Wendy," she said.

They swam over to greet her with kisses.

"I hope you are both ready for practice and exercise," she said to them.

They swam back and forth and came back to her.

"I guess you both are ready then," she said.

Veronica pressed the button to the metal gate. It slid open.

"Okay, Wendy, you first. A few jumps please," Veronica told her.

"Great job, Wendy!" Veronica said.

"Wally, you're next," Veronica told him.

"Let's try tail-walking," she told Wally.

"Great job,Wally!" she said.

Wendy and Wally did more exercises. Then they swam for a while, while Veronica took a break. Later she came back for another half hour of practice with the dolphins.

"Perfect, Wally and Wendy," she told them.

Veronica brought the dolphins in for their meal, then went into the lounge for a break before the show.

She tried to call Marcie but got no answer.

"I guess she never called me about lunch," Veronica told herself.

"Five minutes to show," Hank called to Veronica.

The lights were on the water.

"Ladies and gentlemen, welcome Veronica," Hank announced.

The audience applauded for a few minutes.

Wendy then did three back flips and spins, and Wally did hoop-jumping and tail-walking. The crowd cheered louder.

The show was a big success and soon over.

"Thank you, everyone," Veronica said.

"Wave good-bye to everyone, Wendy and Wally," Veronica said through a microphone.

Veronica was tired and went back to the lounge.

"Thank God I don't have to stay for the next show," she told herself.

She changed, gathered her things and was on her way.

She tried to call Marcie one more time, on her cell phone, but again she got no answer. She left a message.

Veronica finally got to her apartment but found no message from Marcie.

The phone rang. It was Trevor.

"Hi, thought you were Marcie," she told him.

"Sorry to disappoint you," he said.

"No, Trevor, I'm glad you called. I was supposed to meet her for lunch, but she never called me back," Veronica explained.

"Well, I had to call you again. I'm on my way to the airport," he told her.

"Have a safe trip, love," she told him. "Okay, see you in a few days."

She hung up the phone.

Veronica decided it was time to call her parents and tell them about her engagement.

She dialed their number, and her mom picked up the phone.

"Hello, Mom. It's Veronica," she said.

"Hi, Dear How are you?" her mother asked.

"Doing great. I have some news," Veronica said.

"Oh," her mom said.

"Yes, Trevor proposed to me," Veronica told her mom.

"Oh, how exciting! I'm very happy for you, Veronica," her mom said.

"I'll tell your dad. He's not home yet," her mom told her.

"I'll call you in a few days," Veronica said.

"Bye," her mom said.

The phone rang twenty minutes later.

"Hi, dear. It's Mom. Your dad wants to talk to you," she said.

"Hi, Ronnie. Your mom just told me the news. Trevor is a good man," her father told her.

"Thanks, Dad. I'm glad you approve," Veronica said.

"Well, here's Mom," he said.

"Well, Veronica, talk to you soon, I'm going to finish getting dinner ready," her mom told her.

"Okay, I'll talk to you in a few days," Veronica said.

Veronica smiled as she hung up the phone. She kept thinking about she and Trevor saying their "I do's."

Veronica put on her nightie and wanted to relax. It wasn't that late. She wanted to read some of a book she had been putting off. She curled up with a light blanket and started to read. She must have dozed off because the phone woke her up. It was Marcie.

"Hi, Ronnie. Sorry about today," Marcie said.

"It's okay. I was busy doing a show and remembered we had a lunch date," Veronica told her.

"We can make lunch plans next week," Marcie told her.

"Okay, great. Just call me you are free," Veronica said.

She hung up the phone, then went to bed.

Morning came before she knew it. Veronica heard the paperboy. She went to the door to get the paper.

She noticed the front page.

"Wow! Trevor bought a hotel," she said.

He was standing beside it.

"This is exciting," she thought.

Veronica got into the shower and was singing. When she got out, she thought, "Today is going to be a lovely day."

Once Veronica was ready for work, she got in her car and headed to the aquarium. The new seals would be there waiting.

She arrived at the aquarium at 9 a.m. She went to check on the dolphins.

"Good morning, Ronnie," Laura said.

"Morning, Laura, are the seals ready for their training?" Veronica asked.

"Yes, they are ready to go," Laura said.

"Great. Show me where they are," Veronica said.

They walked over to the seal pool.

"Veronica, meet Penny and Pam," Laura said.

They swam over to Veronica.

"Pleased to meet you girls," she said to the seals.

"Penny knows a little more than Pam," Laura told Veronica.

"Well, I'll get started," Veronica said.

As Veronica was finishing up with Penny and Pam, a man walked into the room.

He was tall, had blond hair, and was very attractive and in good shape, she thought.

"Hello, you must be Veronica?" he asked.

"Yes," she answered.

"I'm Samuel, the new trainer," he told her.

"Pleased to meet you, Samuel.

I look forward to working with you," she told him.

"It will be my pleasure to work with such a pretty woman," he told her.

"Well, it's time for my break," she told him.

"Okay, see you later," Samuel said.

Veronica went into the lounge and decided to try to call Trevor to see if he had arrived safely.

She dialed the number.

"Powell International," his secretary answered.

"Hi, Betty. Has Trevor arrived yet?" Veronica asked.

"He just arrived. Hold on a few minutes," Betty told her.

"Hello, is this my beautiful bride to be?" Trevor asked.

"It sure is, my love," she answered.

"I won't keep you. Just wanted to tell you I love you, and congratulations on the hotel. I saw it in the paper this morning," she told him.

"Yes, I was going to surprise you and show you the hotel this weekend," he said to her.

"Well, I have to get to my meeting," he told her.

"I love you, too, Ronnie," he said.

She hung up the phone and changed into her other bathing suit. The show was about to start in fifteen minutes.

The lights were on the water. "Ladies and gentlemen, welcome Veronica," the announcer said.

Riding in a power boat, Veronica stood up and waved. The audience applauded.

Suddenly the crowd stood up to see what had happened: Veronica had fallen out of the boat into the water.

Samuel, who was watching from the side, dived into the water to help her.

He pulled her out and laid her on the tile near the pool. Her head was bleeding.

Someone in the back room called an ambulance. Samuel could hear the sirens.

He gave her mouth-to-mouth resuscitation, and she began coming to. Then the paramedics arrived and took her to the hospital.

Samuel and Laura followed the ambulance to the hospital, where they went to the waiting area.

"I sure hope she's okay," Laura told Samuel.

"She has a nasty bump on her head, and it was bleeding a bit," Samuel said.

"I should try to call her boyfriend, Trevor," Laura said.

Laura came back in five minutes.

"I left a message with his secretary and on his cell phone. Hopefully, he will get it soon," Laura said.

A man walked over to them.

"I'm Dr. Mason. Is Veronica's family here?" he asked.

"Not at the moment. We work with her," Laura told him.

"She needs surgery," the doctor told them.

"I called her sister. She is on her way," Laura said.

"There she is now," Laura said.

Laura saw Veronica's sister walking toward her.

"Hi, Melanie," Laura said.

"Hi, Laura. How is my sister?" Melanie asked.

"She needs surgery," Laura told her.

"Oh no, is it that bad?" Melanie asked.

"Hang on. I'll tell the nurse to tell the doctor you are here," Laura said.

A few minutes later the doctor came out to talk to Melanie. He told her that Veronica had swelling in her eyes.

"We need to operate to get some of the fluid out," he told her.

"Okay, doctor," Melanie said.

"Well, I better get into the operating room. I'll let you know how she is doing as soon as possible," the doctor told her.

"Okay, thank you, doctor," Melanie said.

The nurse came over to Laura.

"There is a phone call for you. It's Trevor Powell," the nurse told her.

Laura walked over to the nurses' station and picked up the phone.

"Hi Trevor. It seems bad. Veronica is in surgery now," she told him.

"Well, I'm at the airport now.

I should be there in a few hours or so," he told her.

Laura hung up the phone.

She walked back to Samuel and Melanie. "He's on his way," she told them.

"I'll call Mom and Dad," Melanie said.

"I'll get some coffee," said Samuel.

When Melanie came back, she was crying. Laura walked over and gave her a hug.

"Your parents coming?" Laura asked.

"Yes, they are. They are very upset," Melanie told Laura.

Samuel came back with the coffee.

"Here you go, Laura. Here's yours, Melanie," he said.

"Thanks, Samuel," they both said.

The nurse came over to them.

"The doctor will be out in a few minutes," she told them.

A few minutes went by before the doctor came over.

"Well, she's out of surgery. She is still asleep," he said.

"Will she be all right?" Melanie asked.

"We don't know yet," the doctor told Melanie.

"Can I see her?" Melanie asked.

"In about an hour," he told her.

"Okay, thank you, Dr. Mason," Melanie said.

"I better get back to the aquarium," Samuel told them.

"Okay, thanks for being here and helping her, Samuel," Melanie said to him.

"Glad I was there to help her," he replied.

"See you at work later, Laura," Samuel said.

"Let's go for a walk outside and get some air," Laura told Melanie.

They walked down the long hallway to the elevator and went outside.

After a while they went to the chapel to say some prayers. They stayed there praying for what seemed a long time. They each lit a candle for Veronica. They both said one last prayer and went back to the waiting area.

"It's been about an hour now," Melanie said to Laura.

Melanie walked over to the nurses' station to ask if she could see Veronica.

"Yes, in five minutes, I'll come get you," the nurse told her.

"Okay, thank you, nurse," Melanie said.

The nurse came back sooner than expected.

"Okay, Melanie, I'll take you in now," the nurse said.

"I'll wait for you, Melanie," Laura told her.

Laura walked outside to make a call on her cell phone. She noticed a man walking toward her.

"Trevor," she said.

"Hi, Laura. How's my Veronica?" he asked.

"She's just out of surgery. Melanie is with her now," she told him.

"I need to see her," he said.

"Okay, let's go talk to the nurse," she told him.

They walked over to the nurses' station. Laura noticed Melanie coming out and crying. Trevor walked over and gave her a hug.

"She's just lying there, all bandaged up," Melanie told them.

"I need to go in and see her," he said.

"Okay, we will wait here," Laura said.

Trevor walked into the room, Veronica was lying so still. Her eyes were bandaged.

"My dear Veronica," he said.

He sat by her bed and held her hand. The nurse came in.

"She should wake up soon," she told him.

"Okay, thank you, nurse," he said.

"My name is Tess," she told him.

"I'm Trevor," he told her.

As he sat there and talked to Veronica and told her he loved her, he had tears in his eyes. He noticed her moving her head.

"Yes, wake up, my dear," he said.

"Veronica, you awake?" he asked.

"Trevor, is that you?" she asked.

"Yes, love, I'm here," he told her.

"Why do I have bandages on my eyes?" she asked.

"You had a bad fall at work," he told her.

"Oh, my God! Am I blind?" she asked.

"I haven't heard anything. The doctor will be back later. Don't worry, Ronnie. I'm here for you," Trevor told her.

"Did you call Mom and Dad?" she asked.

"Yes, they are on their way with Melissa," he told her.

"Melanie is here with Laura in the waiting area," he said.

"Oh, what a big commotion I am causing," she told Trevor.

"No, darling, we all love you, and we want to be here for you," he reassured her.

"I think I will rest some, Trevor. I am very tired," she told him.

"Okay, Ronnie. I'll be back later," he said.

He kissed her on the forehead and then walked back out to Melanie and Laura.

"How is she?" Melanie asked.

"She just woke up. She's very tired. She's worried about being blind," he told them.

"Oh, no," Melanie said.

"No word from the doctor yet?" Trevor asked.

"No, nothing," said Laura.

The nurse overheard them talking and walked over to them.

"The doctor is on his way to talk to you," she said.

"Okay, thank you, Tess," Trevor said.

Trevor paced back and forth, and the girls sat together.

The doctor finally came over to them.

Hi. I'm Dr. Mason," he said to Trevor.

Trevor shook his hand.

"Let me explain what we had to do to Veronica," he said.

"She has swelling in her eyes, lots of fluid, from the fall when she hit her head.

"We did surgery and drained some of it out," he explained.

"Will she be able to see?" Trevor asked.

"In these cases, we don't know. We have to wait. In a few days we can take off the bandages. We'll do more scans," the doctor said.

"Oh, I see," said Trevor.

"Well, I have to get back," the doctor said. "I'll check on her before I leave."

"Thank you, doctor," Trevor said.

Trevor went back and sat by Veronica's bed. He held her hand as she slept soundly.

A nurse came in to check on her.

"You should go, sir. You can come back later," she told him.

"Please call if there are any changes," he said.

Trevor walked out of the room and went to the men's room, where he splashed water on his face. He couldn't believe this had happened to his Veronica.

He walked into the chapel and sat down to pray. After he sat there for a while, he got up and lit a candle, then left the chapel.

The sun was coming up, Trevor felt tired but awake, too. He walked outside to get some air.

He noticed three people walking toward him. They were Veronica's parents and her sister Melissa. He went to greet them.

"Hi Trevor. How is she?" her mom asked.

"She's sleeping now," he told them.

"Can we see her?" her dad asked.

"I'm sure the nurse will let you go in. I'll walk you over to the nurses' station. The nurse's name is Tess."

"Hi, Tess. These are Veronica's parents and her sister. They would like to see her for a few minutes." Trevor told her.

"Sure, I'll take them in," she said.

They all walked into Veronica's room.

I'll leave you alone. I'm going home for a while, I'll be back later," Tess told them.

"Oh my dear, dear girl," her mom said. She kissed Veronica on the cheek and whispered, "I love you" to her.

Veronica must have heard. "Mom, is that you?" she asked.

"Yes, dear, and Dad and Melissa, too," she told Veronica.

"What a way to get some attention!" Veronica told them.

"Well, we are all here for you," her mom told her.

"Dad, you are not saying much," Veronica said.

"I'm here," he told her.

He walked closer to the bed.

"I must look a sight with these bandages all over me," Veronica said.

"Soon they will be off," he told her.

"Where's Trevor?" she asked.

"He went to get some air. He was here all night," her mom said.

"Well, I'm sorry I caused so much trouble for everyone," she told them.

"You'll be better soon, Ronnie," Melissa told her.

"Yes, I will. Don't worry, sweetie," she told her sister.

"We will let you rest a little more, then we will come back in an hour or so, okay, dear?" her mom said.

"I'll be here," Veronica said.

They all kissed her good-bye, then walked out of the room.

Trevor was waiting by the door.

"Let me take you to Ronnie's apartment. You all can freshen up," Trevor suggested.

"Okay, we will follow you," Veronica's dad said.

Her mom, dad, Trevor and Melissa got to the apartment.

Her mom had tears in her eyes. She started picking things up and cleaning a little.

"You don't have to do that, Kate," her husband told her.

"It's okay, Mac. I want to keep busy," she told him.

The phone rang, and Melissa picked it up.

"Hi, this is Marcie. Is Ronnie there?" she asked.

"Hi Marcie. This is Melissa. Ronnie had an accident."

"Oh no, what happened? Is she okay?" Marcie asked.

"She fell at work and hit her head. She needed an eye operation," Melissa explained.

"I'll have to stop by to see her," Marcie said.

"Okay, Marcie. I'll tell Ronnie you were asking for her," Melissa said.

"Okay, hang in there. Tell your family I'm praying for her," Marcie said.

"Mom, that was Marcie. She's going to stop by to see Ronnie," Melissa told her.

"Oh, good. Marcie is a nice girl," her mom said.

Veronica's mom made breakfast for everyone. They ate a little, cleaned the dishes and headed back to the hospital.

It was 9 a.m. when they got back.

Veronica's mom brought some flowers into the room. Melanie was there.

"Hi, Mom," she said as she gave her a hug. "You okay? Melanie asked.

"I've been better, dear," her mother replied.

"She's been sleeping a lot. The doctor is supposed to stop by before he goes home," Melanie said.

"I worry for her so much, Melanie," her mom said.

"She'll be okay, Mom. We'll keep praying," Melanie said.

Veronica moved her head.

"Hey, Ronnie. It's me, your big sister," Melanie said.

"Hi, Mel," Veronica said.

"Mom is here, too," she told her.

"Hi, dear. I brought you some flowers, your favorite, pink roses," Veronica's mother said.

"Oh, yes, I can smell them. Thank you," Veronica said.

"I have a bad headache," she told them.

"I'll go tell the nurse," Melanie said.

"The doctor will be back again, Ronnie," her mom told her.

"I just want to go home," she said.

"Soon, dear," her mom told her.

Melanie came back.

"The nurse will be in with some medication for your headache," Melanie told Veronica.

After a few minutes, the nurse walked into the room with the doctor.

"Hi, Veronica. I'm Dr. Mason," he told her.

"Hi, doctor," she replied.

"How are you feeling today?" he asked.

"I have a headache," she told him.

The nurse gave her two pills.

"This should help," she told Veronica.

Dr. Mason explained to Veronica, her mom and sister that they would be taking her in for more tests to check to see if the swelling had gone down.

"The nurse will get you ready to go down, okay, Veronica?" he said.

"Okay, yes," she said.

"Where are Dad and Trevor?" she asked.

"They went for a walk, Ronnie," her mom said.

"I'll be right back for you, Veronica," the nurse told her.

"I like that nurse Tess; wish she were on," Veronica said.

"She was on early this morning. She said she was going home and would be on later," Veronica's mom said.

"I'm scared, Mom," Veronica said.

"It's okay, dear. We will wait for you right here," her mom and Melanie told her.

"We are here for you every step of the way," her mom said with tears in her eyes.

Trevor and her dad came into the room.

"Hello, young lady," her dad said.

"I'm going down for some tests, but I'll be back soon," Veronica told her dad.

The nurse brought in a wheelchair and helped Veronica into it.

"I'll be back in no time," she told everyone.

"Did Melissa get back yet?" her mom asked.

"We dropped her off at the aquarium. She's driving Ronnie's car here," Trevor said.

"Let's all go out for some air while we wait for Ronnie," Trevor suggested.

Melissa pulled into the hospital parking lot. Trevor noticed her. As she walked closer to everyone, they could see she had been crying. Trevor walked over to her.

"Don't worry, Melissa. Your sister will be back to normal in no time," he told her.

"I sure hope so, Trevor," a tearful Melissa said.

"I'm going to the gift shop to get Ronnie a special gift," Melissa told everyone.

"I'll go with you, honey," her mom said.

A half hour later Melissa and her mom came back.

"I found the perfect gift. It's a glass cross with a rose inside," she said as she showed it to everyone.

"It's beautiful. She'll love it," said Melanie.

"Wonder what's taking so long with the test? It's almost noon," Trevor said.

Trevor went to the nurses' station, where Tess was just coming on duty again.

"Hi, Tess. Just checking on Veronica and her test," he said.

"I'll check for you. Give me a few minutes. It shouldn't be much longer," she told him.

Trevor walked back to everyone.

"She should be back soon," he told them.

As Trevor waited by the door, the nurse brought Veronica back in a wheelchair.

"Hi, love," Trevor said.

"Hi, Trevor, you been waiting all this time?" she asked.

"Yes, I will always wait for you," he told her.

Tess came into the room.

"The doctor wants to talk to all of you. He'll be down shortly," she said.

Trevor went to get Veronica's parents, and they all waited in the room with Veronica.

"Everyone is so quiet," Veronica said.

"We just want the results," Trevor told her.

"Where's Melissa?" Veronica asked.

"She's with Melanie. They'll be here soon," her mom said.

Tess came in with Dr. Mason.

Hello again, everyone. We have some good news. The swelling has gone down, most of it," he told them.

"What about my eyesight?" Veronica asked.

"The bandages come off in a few days. We have to wait and see what happens. It could be your eyesight could come back slowly. We'll be able to tell more in a few days," the doctor said.

"I'll be back tomorrow to check on you, Veronica," he added. "Well, thank you, Dr. Mason," Trevor said as they shook hands.

"At least we know something," her mom said.

"Why don't you all go to lunch? I want to rest some more," Veronica said.

"You sure you want us to go?" her mom asked.

"Yes, go," Veronica told them.

Her mom kissed her good-bye, then they left.

Veronica lay in the bed. Tears rolled down her cheeks. She cried herself to sleep.

After 4 p.m. when Trevor and her parents came back, Veronica was still sleeping.

Marcie came into the room.

"Hi, Marcie," Veronica's mom said.

"Hi, everyone. How is she doing?" Marcie asked.

"She's doing okay, I guess," her mom told Marcie.

Marcie gave Veronica's mom a big hug.

"We are glad you are here, Marcie," they all said.

Veronica was waking up.

"Hi, dear. We are all here," her mom said.

"Did you all go to lunch?" Veronica asked.

"Yes, dear, it's after 4 p.m. Marcie is here, too," her mom said.

"Hi, Marcie," said Veronica. "I'm thirsty."

"Hold on. I'll get you some water," Veronica's mom said.

About that time Tess came in and told everyone Veronica needed rest.

They all said their good-byes and left.

"See you tomorrow," they all said.

Tess checked Veronica's bandages and noticed she had been crying.

"I know we don't know each other very well, but if you ever need to talk, I'll listen," Tess told her.

"Okay, thank you, Tess," Veronica said.

The next two nights, Tess was by Veronica's side. Tess talked to her, cried with her, listened to her, and held her hand.

The morning came for the bandages to come off. When Veronica woke up, it was early and she was alone in her room.

She said a prayer to herself:

"Dear God, "Please get me through this struggle, and give me strength. Amen." Thank you, dear Lord," she said.

The hospital staff brought in her breakfast and set it on her table.

The nurse came in, and Veronica told her she wasn't hungry.

"Well, have some juice at least," the nurse said.

"Okay, I'll have some juice," Veronica said and took a sip.

"Are you nervous, Veronica?" the nurse asked.

"Yes, I really am. My life will be so different if I am blind," she replied. "I know it's early, but do you want me to call your family?" the nurse asked.

"No, I'm sure they will be here soon," Veronica said. "I just have to wait for the doctor and the results," she said.

"Well, I'll see you later," the nurse said.

Veronica finished drinking her juice, then tried to rest some more, but she couldn't sleep. "I just want this over with," she told herself.

It seemed like a long while before the doctor finally came.

"Good morning, Veronica," he said.

Tess was with him.

"You are still here, Tess?" Veronica said.

"Yes, I'll go home soon, just wanted to be here to help you out," she told Veronica.

"Thanks. That means a lot to me," Veronica said.

"Any headaches this morning?" Dr. Mason asked.

"Just a little one," she told him.

"Well, let's take these bandages off and see what is going on," he told her.

"It could take awhile before we know anything for sure. You'll have to use these dark glasses," the doctor told her.

He took the bandages off, a little at a time.

"Okay, keep your eyes closed," he told her.

He took out a little light.

"Now, open them slowly please," he said.

Veronica opened her eyes but saw nothing.

The doctor checked her pupils.

"We'll do more tests in an hour. I'll go set it up now. Hang in there," he told her.

Veronica was crying. Tess sat by her and held her hand.

She handed Veronica the glasses and said, "Put these on.

"Let me finish up some other work, then I'll come back to take you to get your tests," Tess said.

"I thought you were supposed to go home soon," Veronica said.

"I'll do this, then I will go," Tess said.

"Thanks, Tess. You're a good nurse," Veronica told her.

Trevor came into the room as Veronica was just dozing off. He sat in a chair and watched her.

He noticed the bandages were gone, replaced by patches on her eyes and dark glasses on the table.

She began to wake up again.

"Veronica, my love, it's Trevor. Any news?" he asked.

"I can't see, not sure why. They are taking me for more tests," she told him.

Tears streamed down her face.

"Don't worry, honey. I'll get you the best treatment," he told her.

"I need some time alone to think things through. A lot has happened," Veronica told him.

"Ronnie, what are you saying?" Trevor asked.

"Give me a few weeks to see how I feel and if I get my sight back," she told him.

"I'm not giving up on you. I love you," he said to her.

"I'll call you in a few weeks," she told him.

He kissed her on the cheek and left.

Veronica cried.

She didn't want him to go but told herself, "I don't know what to do."

Tess came back to take Veronica to get her tests.

"You okay?" Tess asked.

"Not really," Veronica said.

She put her hands over her face and couldn't stop crying.

"You want to talk about it?" Tess asked.

"Thanks, but maybe another time," Veronica told her.

Tess helped her into the wheelchair.

"Let's get these tests done," Tess said to her.

When Veronica got back from her tests, her parents were waiting for her.

"We ran into Trevor a few minutes ago. He seemed upset," her mom said.

"I told him I need some time alone to think about things. Since I can't see at the moment, I don't want to be a burden to anyone," she told them.

"You are not a burden to anyone, dear. We all love you and want to help you," they both explained.

"Hand me my dark glasses please," Veronica said.

"I want to rest some, Mom and Dad. We can talk tomorrow," she told them.

Her mom and dad said good-bye to her and left. Tess came in.

"Hi, Veronica," she said.

"No more tests; I'm tired," Veronica told Tess.

"No, Marcie is here to see you," Tess told her.

"Tell her I am very tired. I'll talk to her tomorrow," Veronica said. "I just want to be alone."

"C'mon, Ronnie, it's me, your best friend. Talk to me," Marcie said.

"What's there to talk about? I'm blind; that's that," Veronica told her.

"They have places you can go, so you can learn to live being blind," Marcie told her.

"Well, I'm not going anywhere," Veronica told her.

"They have seeing-eye dogs. It would take a month for you to learn," Tess told her.

"When you come back home, you can stay with me," Marcie told Veronica.

"Leave me alone," Veronica said to her.

"Okay, fine, but I won't give up on you," Marcie told her.

She touched her shoulder and left.

Tess brought in Veronica's lunch. "Are you hungry at all," she asked Veronica.

"No, I'm not," Veronica said.

"Let's talk then," Tess said.

"Why, what good will that do?" Veronica asked.

"Tell me what you are feeling," Tess said and closed the door.

"I know this is a very big change in your life, and it is very confusing for you," Tess told her.

"It's very scary," Veronica said. "I know it's scary," Tess told her.

"I don't want to take time away from you or your family, Tess," Veronica said.

"You are not. I'm not married. I just broke up with someone," Tess told her.

"I know the feeling. I canceled my engagement to Trevor," Veronica told her.

"Sorry to hear that. He seems like a nice man," Tess told her.

"Sorry about your breakup, too, Tess," Veronica said.

"Maybe we both can cry over coffee sometime," Tess told her.

"Sure," Veronica said.

"I'm here if you need me. Okay, Veronica?" Tess said.

"Thanks. You are so easy to talk to," Veronica told her.

"Let me get back to work, then I'll come before I go home," Tess said.

For some reason Veronica felt better, thanks to Tess, she thought.

She finished her juice and the rest of her soup but spilled a little on her nightie. A man came in to get her tray.

Later Tess came back.

"Before I go, I've got some good news: You get to get out of here Friday," Tess told her.

"I do," a surprised Veronica said.

"They want to send you to the blind institute in Connecticut," Tess told her.

"Well, I guess if I have to go, I will go," Veronica said.

"I can go with you Friday, if you like," Tess said.

"I would like that if you could, Tess," Veronica said to her.

"Good, then it is settled," Tess told her.

Friday came fast. Veronica's parents came to say good-bye, with Melissa. Melanie was there too.

"Good luck, dear. We all will miss you and be thinking of you," Veronica's mom told her.

"See you soon, sis," Melanie said.

Everyone was there except Trevor. Veronica felt badly over the way she had treated him and wished she could see him before she left.

"Okay, Veronica, let's get going," Tess said.

Tess helped her into a wheelchair and carried her bag out.

Veronica cried as Tess wheeled her to the elevator.

The drive was a long one.

They stopped for a bathroom break and a snack.

"Now entering WINSTON, CONNECTICUT," the sign read.

"We will be there shortly," Tess told her.

"I'm very nervous," Veronica said.

"It will be okay. I'm allowed to stay the first night with you," Tess told her.

Tess pulled into the long driveway. She described the place to Veronica.

"It is a big colonial-style building with big white columns. It has lots of trees and grass on 100 acres," Tess told her.

"Sounds beautiful," Veronica said.

Tess turned off the car.

"Are you ready?" Tess asked.

"Ready as ever," Veronica told her.

They walked into the building.

Tess helped Veronica sit down in the living area.

It had floral wallpaper and a maroon couch and chairs.

I'll be right back, Veronica," Tess told her.

I'll be here," Veronica said.

Tess came back a few minutes later with the director.

"Veronica, this is Mrs. O'Neill," Tess introduced her.

"Pleased to meet you," Veronica said.

"Welcome. Let me show you to your room, and we can go over some of the things later," Mrs. O'Neill said.

As they walked down a long hallway, Veronica held on to Tess' arm.

"Soon you will be walking all by yourself," Tess told her.

Veronica agreed and smiled.

"I will let you both get settled. Then we will talk about what you will be learning," Mrs. O'Neill told Veronica.

"Thank you," she said.

"This room isn't so bad," Tess told her.

"I can't see it, so it doesn't matter," Veronica said.

"I can tell you are nervous by the tone of your voice," Tess said.

"I know. I'm sorry. You have been so good to me, putting up with my moods," Veronica said.

"Well, I consider you my friend," Tess told her.

"The feeling is mutual, Tess," Veronica said.

Mrs. O'Neill came into the room to get Veronica for a group session.

"You can come, too, Tess," she told her.

Tess was going to help Veronica walk to the room.

"Use this walking stick, Veronica. You will have to get used to it," Mrs. O'Neill told her.

Tess walked to Veronica's left. Veronica counted the steps as she walked.

"Here we are," Tess told her.

Tess looked around as they walked into the room. There were about 25 people in the room. Everyone sat in a circle and introduced themselves. A few, like Veronica, had a nurse with them.

Mrs. O'Neill and an instructor discussed the schedule and learning process for them.

"We are all going to walk outside around the yard," the instructor told them.

They all got in a line, one at a time.

Tess stayed in the room with the other nurses.

An hour later they all came back, and Veronica sat down.

"You okay, Veronica?" Tess asked.

"Yes, it's just frustrating, I hate this," she said loudly.

"Calm down. It's okay," Tess told her. Tess leaned over and gave her a hug.

"I'm sorry, Tess. This is just hard for me," Veronica said.

"I'll ask Mrs. O'Neill if I can stay an extra night," Tess said.

"You would do that for me?" Veronica asked.

"Yes, we are friends," Tess told her.

"Thanks," Veronica said.

"Mrs. O'Neil told everyone they could go back to their rooms for a while, until the next lesson began.

Veronica was glad. She just wanted to lie down.

Tess woke Veronica up an hour later.

"Wake up, hon. You have more training in a half hour," Tess told her.

"I can't do this. It's too hard for me," Veronica told Tess.

"Yes, you can do this. I will help you all I can," Tess said.

"C'mon let's go," Tess said.

Veronica reluctantly got up.

Everyone was already in the room when Veronica and Tess got there.

With Tess' help, Veronica sat in the last seat, in the end row.

The instructor brought in a seeing-eye dog named Ruby.

Glenn was the instructor's name. He had Ruby and the dog's owner demonstrate some small tasks.

"It seems hard right now, but you will get the hang of it," Glenn told the group. "Tomorrow you will have practice with Ruby."

After the session, they all went back to their rooms to get ready for dinner.

"Did you ask Mrs. O'Neill if you could stay two nights?" Veronica asked Tess.

"I explained to her how you were feeling. She said just one extra night, then I have to go," Tess said.

"I'll miss you when you go, Tess," Veronica told her.

"I'll see you when you get back. We will have lunch then," Tess told her.

"Let's get ready for dinner. They are having spaghetti," Tess told Veronica.

"Mmmm, my favorite," said Veronica.

As they walked down the hall to the dining room, Veronica tripped and fell.

"You okay, hon?" Tess asked.

"Yes, I'm just clumsy," Veronica said.

The dining room was getting full, but they found a seat.

They had salad, spaghetti, and garlic bread. For dessert they had chocolate pudding.

After dinner everyone went to the room, to group talk.

Veronica talked a little bit. She cried some.

When the group discussion was over, Tess and Veronica went for a walk outside. They stopped and sat on a bench near the garden.

Veronica couldn't get used to the idea of being blind.

"I can't do this, Tess. I need to go home," Veronica said.

"You have to stay here and learn to get through this," Tess told her in a different tone.

"Veronica, it's your challenge. Only you can do this. No one else can," Tess told her again.

Veronica was silent for a few minutes, then wanted to go back to her room. Walking with her, Tess tried to comfort her.

"I should go home. I'm distracting you by being here.

I'm babying you. You have to do this on your own. I'll leave in the morning," Tess told her.

"Please don't go, Tess. I'll try; I will," Veronica told her.

"I'll leave early and will pick you up in three weeks," Tess said.

Tess woke up early the next morning, packed her small bag and got ready to go. She said goodbye to Veronica and hugged her.

"See you soon, Veronica. You can do this," Tess told her.

Later, Veronica thought about what Tess had told her. She did try harder and was learning to cope. After all, she wasn't the only blind person at the school.

As the weeks went by, Veronica got her own dog, a golden retriever named Shelby. They were good together.

The weeks passed quickly. Her parents called, and friends called, but Trevor never did.

Veronica thought, "Why would he call?" After all, she had told him to go away. Now, she wished she hadn't done that.

The day finally came to go home.

Veronica was getting around so well. Shelby was always by her side. They got around almost anywhere. She was walking on the grounds when she heard a familiar voice.

"Well, look at you, Veronica. You are like a pro." It was Tess talking.

"Hi, Tess, can you believe this? I'm getting around pretty well. This is my pal and helper Shelby," she said.

"Hi there, Shelby," Tess said.

He raised his paw and touched Tess' hand.

"So, you ready to get back home?" Tess asked Veronica.

"I sure am," Veronica said.

Veronica said good-bye to the people and the staff and thanked everyone. Tess helped her in the car with Shelby, and they drove off.

"It's good to talk to you again, Tess. I missed you," Veronica told her.

"I missed you, too," Tess said.

It took them about four hours to get back, partly because they took a few breaks and talked a bit.

As Tess pulled up to Veronica's apartment, she said, "Veronica, I have something to ask you."

"Yes," Veronica said.

"I have a guest house you could stay in. It has more room for you than your apartment and a big yard for Shelby. If you want, we can move you there," Tess told her.

"I would never want to impose on you, Tess," Veronica said.

"You won't be imposing. My brother will help us move you in," Tess said.

"Sure, Tess, why not?" Veronica agreed: "Then it is set. I'll call my brother and let him know," Tess said.

"I'm going to go now. Do you need anything or want me to stay?" Tess asked.

"No, I'm fine. I'm sure my mom will call me later," Veronica said.

"Okay, if you need anything, just call me, I'll pick you up tomorrow, sometime after 1 p.m."

"Okay, thanks again, Tess," Veronica said.

It seemed strange to Veronica to be in her apartment again. She sat in the chair by the window as Shelby lay beside her.

The phone rang. She had the cordless phone near her. I was her mom. "Hi, Mom," she said.

"Hi dear. Tess called me and told me she dropped you off," her mom said.

"I'm sitting in my chair with Shelby next to me on the floor," she told her mom.

"Did you have dinner?" her mom asked.

"Yes, I had some soup and a sandwich. I'm going to bed early anyway," Veronica said.

"Well, I'll call you tomorrow," her mom told her.

"Okay, mom, love you," she said and hung up the phone.

"Let's get ready for bed, Shelby," Veronica told him.

He stood right up and guided her to the room.

The next morning Veronica was awakened by chirping birds. It seemed as if it would be a nice day. She got up to use the bathroom, then went into the kitchen.

She remembered where some things were, but she also became confused at times.

Shelby wanted to go out, so they walked slowly around the block. When they got back, Shelby let Veronica know that she had a message on her machine. It was Tess. She had said she would be there by 9 a.m. to pack her things.

Tess also said her brother and his friend would be there by 10 a.m. to start moving her furniture and other things in a truck.

Veronica was both excited and nervous.

With Shelby directing her steps, Veronica walked to the bathroom to take a shower. Shelby waited by the door.

When Veronica later turned off the shower, she heard something.

"Hello," she said.

Veronica took Shelby's leash and walked out of the room. She had on just a towel.

"It's me, Tess. The door was unlocked, so I came in."

"Oh okay. I was just getting out of the shower," Veronica told her.

"I can see that," Tess said.

"Let me get dressed," Veronica said.

"I brought some boxes for your things. I'll start packing the stuff in the living room," Tess told her.

"Wish I could help, but you know I'm blind," she said. They both laughed.

"My brother Gregg should be here soon, with his friend Ben," Tess told her.

"Well, thanks for all your help," Veronica said.

Gregg and Ben arrived a half hour after Tess did.

She introduced them to each other. Then they started moving Veronica's furniture to the truck.

Veronica tried to help pack but wasn't much help.

Gregg and Ben took the first truckload to the guest house.

When the men came back for the last of the boxes, Tess, Veronica and Shelby got in the car and were on their way to Veronica's new place.

"So, you sure this is okay, me staying at the guest house, Tess?" Veronica asked.

"Yes, it's perfectly fine. I want you to stay there. No more talk about that," Tess told her.

"Okay, I won't say another word about it," Veronica said.

They pulled into a circular driveway.

"Well, here we are, home sweet guest home," Tess said. Veronica laughed.

Tess helped her out of the car, and Shelby was by her side, too.

"You and Shelby walk a little. I'll get some stuff in your new place," Tess told her.

"Thanks again, Tess," Veronica said.

She gave Tess a hug.

Veronica and Shelby walked for a while, then found a bench to sit on. She could hear the truck pulling in one last time. The sun felt warm on her face.

"Veronica," Tess called. "I made up some lunch if you are hungry."

"Okay, thanks. I'll be right there," she told Tess.

Veronica and Shelby walked to the door. When Veronica walked inside, everyone yelled, "Surprise!"

"What's going on?" Veronica asked with a smile.

"We are welcoming you home," Tess told her.

Veronica's mom and dad were there. So were, her sisters, Melanie and Melissa. Laura and Samuel came from work. Marcie came, too.

"Is Trevor here?" Veronica asked.

"No, he's not here," her mom said.

"We tried to call him, but he didn't answer our calls," Tess told her.

"Maybe he's working on his new hotel," Veronica said.

"Well, we are glad you are home, Ronnie," Melissa told her.

"Yes, it's good to be here with all of you," she told them.

"When did you all plan this?" Veronica asked.

"When you were in Connecticut," Tess told her.

"Well, it sure was a nice surprise," Veronica told everyone.

"You deserve it," said Tess.

"So Laura, how are Wendy and Wally doing?" Veronica asked.

"They are doing very well. Samuel is taking great care of them. You should stop by and say hello to them. I know they miss you," Laura told her.

"Sure, I'd love to come by," Veronica told her.

"How about next week? We'll set something up," Laura said.

"Yes, okay," said Veronica.

Veronica's mom brought out a cake for her. I know you can't see it, dear, but it's chocolate with butter cream frosting.

It says: "WELCOME HOME, RONNIE," and it's decorated with pink roses.

"Thanks, Mom, I'll have a big piece please," Veronica said.

They were all talking and enjoying their dessert, when the phone rang.

"Veronica, it's for you. It's Trevor," her mom told her.

"Hello," she said softly.

"Hi, Veronica. I got a few messages from your mom and Tess," he said.

"How have you been?" she asked him.

"Actually, I just got back in town an hour ago," he told her.

"Maybe we can get some lunch next week," she said.

"Sure, if I'm free, how are you feeling?" he asked.

"Pretty good, other than I can't see. I have Shelby. He helps me get around a lot," she told Trevor.

"Well, I look forward to seeing you next week. If you need anything, let me know," Trevor told her.

"Thanks," she said.

Veronica's mom took the phone.

"Is everything okay, dear?" she asked.

"Yes, Mom, everything is fine," she said.

"Do you all mind if I go take a nap? You all don't have to leave. I just want to nap for a half hour," Veronica told them.

Tess walked with Veronica and Shelby to the guest house.

"You okay, hon?" Tess asked.

"I'm just emotional; that's all," Veronica told her.

"Okay, I'll come back in an hour, to see how you are feeling. If you want to talk, we can," Tess said.

Veronica gave Tess another hug.

"What was that for?" Tess asked.

"You are a great woman," Veronica told her.

"So are you, Veronica. See you in a little bit," Tess said.

Tess went back to the house and visited with everyone. She talked with Veronica's mom.

"How do you think she is handling being blind?" her mom asked.

"I think she is coping with it. It is a different life for her now. I told her I am here for her if she needs me," Tess said.

"She's very lucky to have you as a friend," her mom said.

"I'm glad she is my friend, too," Tess said.

"I'll go back and check on her, see if she wants to come back over," Tess told everyone.

Tess walked over to the guest house. She called Veronica's name as she walked into the bedroom.

"Veronica, are you awake?" Tess asked.

"Yes," she said.

Veronica was sitting up. Tears were in her eyes.

"Do you want me to tell everyone good-bye for you?" Tess asked her.

"No, just stay with me for a few minutes," Veronica said.

"Okay, I'm here, Veronica," she told her.

"Can I ask you a question?" Veronica said.

"Sure, anything you want to ask me, I'll answer," Tess told her.

"I was just wondering. Was your relationship with a man or a woman?" Veronica asked.

"It was with a woman," Tess told her.

"Really," Veronica said.

"Yes, for five years," Tess said.

"I don't mean to pry. I was just wondering," Veronica told her.

"It's okay. Ask me anything you want," Tess said.

"You must miss her. Five years is a long time," Veronica said.

"I do miss her. I still love here," Tess said to Veronica.

"If you ever want to talk about it, I will listen. Oh, and by the way, call me Ronnie. Veronica seems so formal," she told Tess.

"It's a deal, Ronnie," Tess said.

"Let's go say good-bye," Tess told her.

They walked over to the house. Veronica walked in first, then Tess. I just wanted to thank everyone for the nice surprise today," Veronica said.

"It was our pleasure," they told her.

"It was good to see you, Ronnie. I'll come by next week and pick you up so you can see Wally and Wendy," Laura told her. Then, Laura said, "Why wait? I'll bring you by tomorrow if it's okay."

"Sure, I'd love to," Veronica said.

"I'll be here around noon," Laura told her.

"Okay, bye, Laura; bye, Samuel," she said.

Marcie gave Veronica a hug and left, too.

Veronica's mom stayed for a while longer, talked to her about Trevor, and then left with her dad.

"The time flew by today," Tess told Veronica.

"I'm glad they are gone. I can relax now," Veronica told Tess.

"Do we have any wine left?" she asked Tess.

"Yes, would you like a glass?" Tess asked her.

"I sure would," she said.

"Coming right up. I will join you," Tess said.

Tess brought over two glasses of wine and sat down with Veronica.

"If you don't mind me asking, how was it talking to Trevor today?" Tess asked.

"It was okay. I wanted to talk to him. I still have mixed feelings about him and me," she told Tess.

"He wants to talk next week again," she said.

"Well, I hope everything works out for you, Ronnie. You are a good woman," Tess told her.

"How about you, Tess? How are you doing with your breakup?" Veronica asked her.

"I have good days and bad days, as anyone would," Tess told her.

"Well, I hope, things will work out for you and you find someone new," Veronica told her.

"I'm here to talk to you as you are for me," Veronica told her.

"Well, that means a lot to me," Tess said to Veronica.

Tess touched Veronica's shoulder.

"You okay, Tess?" Veronica asked.

"Yes, I'm sorry. I should get cleaning up," Tess said.

"I'll go back to the guest house," Veronica said.

"No, you don't have to," Tess said.

"I'm tired. I'll see you in the morning, Tess," Veronica said.

"Okay, good night, Ronnie," Tess said.

Veronica and Shelby walked to the guest house.

Shelby woke Veronica up to the sound of rain on the window. Then, they walked outside for a few minutes before coming back inside.

Tess called and asked her to join her for breakfast.

"Do I smell blueberry muffins?" Veronica asked as she and Shelby entered Veronica's house.

"Yes, just out of the oven," Tess told her.

"Sorry I went to bed so early last night," Veronica told Tess.

"It's okay. I understand."

"So is Laura picking you up today?" Tess asked.

"Yes, I am anxious to go to the aquarium to see Wally and Wendy," she said.

"Well, have a good day, Ronnie. I'll be home around 4 this afternoon," Tess told her. "We can have dinner tonight if you want, Ronnie."

"Okay, sounds good," Veronica said.

Veronica heard a car pull up and the doorbell ring.

"Door's open," Veronica yelled.

"Hey, Ronnie, it's me," Laura said.

"Is it that time already?" Veronica said.

"Yes, you ready to go?" Laura asked.

Veronica called Shelby over, and he came running to her.

They got in the car, and Laura drove off.

They were at the aquarium in a half hour.

"Here we are, Ronnie," Laura said.

"I miss being here," Veronica told her.

"We miss you. The dolphins and sea lions miss you, too," Laura said.

As they walked into the building, Shelby guided Veronica, and Laura walked ahead of them.

They stopped and said hello to Hank, Sonny, and Samuel.

They walked up to the dolphin pool, and Veronica stood there with Shelby.

Laura called Wally and Wendy over.

"Say hello to them, Ronnie," Laura told her.

"Hello, Wally, Hello, Wendy."

The dolphins recognized Veronica's voice. They swam back and forth and did flips for her. She could hear the water splashing.

"Oh, I missed you both, too," she told them. Veronica seemed sad.

"You okay, Ronnie?" Laura asked.

"It's just hard to be here and not being able to see," she said.

"I'm so sorry. We will go," Laura said.

"Okay," Veronica agreed.

They walked back to the car and sat there for a few minutes.

"I'm sorry, Laura. You were nice enough to bring me, and I got upset," Veronica said.

"I didn't mean to upset you, Ronnie," Laura told her.

"I just miss working," Veronica said.

"Maybe there is some work you can do here," Laura suggested.

"What would I do?" she asked.

"I'll think of something for you," Laura told her.

"Great! Thanks, Laura," Veronica said.

"Let me get you back home," Laura told her.

Pulling into the driveway, Laura said, "Here we are."

Laura opened the door. Shelby jumped out first and waited for Veronica.

"You need anything?" Laura asked her.

"No, I'm fine. Thanks for the burger," Veronica said.

"Anytime. I'll call you tomorrow about the work situation," Laura said to her.

"Okay, talk to you then," she said.

Laura drove off, and Veronica walked to the guest house.

The phone rang as she walked inside. She picked it up.

"Hello," she said.

"Hi, Ronnie. It's me, Trevor.

"I know I said I would call you later this week, but I need to see you and talk to you," he told her.

"Why, what's wrong?" she asked.

"I miss you. I need to be with you," he told her.

"I can't right now. Trevor. But we can talk," she said.

"I'll be there in an hour," he told her.

Okay," she said.

Veronica lay down on the couch and waited for Trevor. Shelby's barking woke her up. There was a knock at the door.

"Come in. It's open," she said.

"Hi, Ronnie," he said.

"That was fast getting here," she told him.

"I couldn't wait to see you," he told her.

He bent down and kissed her cheek.

"May I sit here next to you?" he asked.

"Sure," she said.

"So what did you want to talk about?" Veronica asked.

"I want us back together," he told her.

"It's hard right now, Trevor. I can't be a burden to you," she told him.

"I told you, honey, you are not a burden. I love you Ronnie. I want you as my wife," he told her.

"I can't marry you, Trevor, not now. I need to get my life in order," she told him.

"So this is it. We are over?" he said.

"Yes, I am sorry. Please don't hate me," she said.

"I could never hate you, Ronnie, I'll always love you," he told her.

"Remember what we used to say to each other?" Veronica asked him.

"I remember," he said.

"Say it," she said.

"Hey," he said.

"Hay is for horses and cows," she said.

"And I love you, too."

Veronica kissed Trevor and told him he had better go.

He touched her face and left.

Veronica cried as Shelby sat beside her.

Veronica heard a car. It must be Tess, she thought, and wiped her tears.

A few minutes later, the phone rang.

"Hello," she answered.

"Hi, Ronnie. I'm home now. We still on for dinner?" Tess asked.

"Sure, I'm looking forward to it," Veronica told her.

"What's wrong? You sound sad," Tess said.

"Oh, Trevor was here. I broke off the engagement, with him," she told Tess.

"Oh, I'm sorry. If you want to cancel dinner, it's okay," Tess told her.

"No, I don't want to be alone," Veronica told her.

"Okay, let me do a few things, then I'll come over and get you," Tess said.

"Okay, Tess, take your time," she said.

Veronica sat on the porch with Shelby. She thought about Trevor and how things happen in an instant. She wished things were different and the accident had never happened. "But this is the way it had to be," she thought.

Tess was outside walking to get Veronica.

"Hey, Ronnie, I'll meet you halfway," Tess yelled to her.

"Okay," she laughed.

They walked toward each other. and Tess gave Veronica a hug.

"Are you okay?" Tess asked.

"I guess so," she said.

"Well, come in the house and have a glass of wine," Tess told her.

They walked into the house.

"Something smells real good," Veronica said.

"I'm making baked scallops," Tess told her.

Veronica sat on the couch, Tess brought her a glass of white wine.

"I'll finish the salad. Then, I'll sit with you for a few minutes while the dinner is cooking," Tess told her.

"I wish I could help. I feel useless," Veronica told her.

It's okay, Ronnie. Just relax," Tess said.

Tess sat down beside Veronica.

"A toast, to new things in life," Tess said.

"I'm glad you are here, Tess. You always make me feel better," Veronica told her.

"So do you want to talk about Trevor, or want me to mind my own business?" Tess asked.

"We can talk about it. I don't mind," Veronica said.

"Tell me how you are feeling right now," Tess said.

"I feel sad but a little relieved. Is it bad to feel that way?" she asked.

"No, I felt that way, too, when I had my breakup," Tess told her.

"I just need to figure things out and learn to live being blind. I don't want pity from anyone," Veronica said.

"Well, you have no pity from me, and you can stay here as long as you want," Tess told her.

"Thanks, Tess," Veronica said.

"Well, let me check on the scallops," Tess said.

"Okay, Ronnie, they are ready," Tess said later.

"Good, I'm hungry," Veronica said.

"Well, I hope you like my cooking," Tess said.

"Let me have a taste and see," Veronica told her.

Tess sat and watched Veronica.

"Well, how is it?" she asked.

"Very good, melts in your mouth, very tasty," Veronica told her.

"Good, glad you like it," Tess said.

"So, how was your day, Tess?" Veronica asked.

"It was busy, went by fast. I kept thinking about our dinner," she said. "Really? I did, too," Veronica told her.

"I guess we were thinking of each other," Tess said.

"Can I ask you something?" Veronica said.

"Sure, ask me anything," Tess said.

"What's it like being with another woman, if it's not too personal to answer?" Veronica asked.

"It's wonderful. If you find someone you love, it's special and very gentle," Tess told her.

"Sorry for being so personal," Veronica said.

"It's okay, Ronnie," she said.

"How about dessert, cheesecake, with strawberries?" Tess said.

"In a few minutes. Let me rest my belly," Veronica said.

"That was a real good dinner, Tess. Sit with me for a few minutes," Veronica told her.

"Okay, just a few minutes. Then I will clean up," Tess told her.

"Laura picked me up today, and we went to the aquarium," Veronica told her.

"Oh, yes, how did that go?" Tess asked.

"It was good. Laura is going to find me some work to do there. Not sure what it will be, but something," Veronica told her.

"That's good to hear," Tess said.

"What do you look like, Tess?" Veronica asked.

"Here, touch my face," Tess told her.

Veronica put her hand on Tess' face. She moved her fingers over Tess' nose, lips, and chin.

"You have soft skin," Veronica told her.

"Thanks, hon. So do you," Tess said.

"What's it like?" Veronica asked.

"What's what like?" Tess said.

"To kiss a woman," Veronica said.

"I better get these dishes done," Tess said.

"I'm sorry. I didn't realize I said that," said Veronica.

"It's okay," Tess said.

"Do you want me to leave?" Veronica said.

"No, stay, unless you want to go," Tess said.

"I want to stay," Veronica told her.

"Let me clean up. Then we will talk some more," Tess told her.

Veronica got up and walked over to Tess, put her hand on Tess' face again, touched her lips and kissed her gently.

"Veronica, you don't know what you are doing." Tess told her.

"Yes, I do. I want this. I have feelings for you. I never felt like this before," she told Tess.

"Please kiss me, Tess, I just want to feel it. I know I will love it," Veronica said.

"I don't know," said Tess.

"Just one time, please," Veronica said.

Tess kissed Veronica softly on the mouth. It felt good to both of them.

"See, Tess, I told you I would like it," Veronica said.

"Maybe you should go back to the cottage," Tess told her.

"Why did I do something wrong?" Veronica asked.

"It's just I don't want to start anything that would confuse you," Tess told her.

"I'm not confused. I really like you," she said.

"We can talk about this in the morning," Tess said.

"Okay, I'm sorry if I did wrong. Please forgive me," Veronica said.

"It's not you, hon," Tess told her.

"Good night, Tess," Veronica said.

"Good night, Ronnie. Sweet dreams," Tess told her.

Veronica took Shelby and walked out the door.

Shelby woke Veronica up the next morning. It seemed very quiet. She didn't hear a thing.

Veronica and Shelby were walking out the door when the phone rang.

"Hello," Veronica said.

"Hi, Ronnie. Do you want to try to come in today to work? You can do some announcing," Laura said.

"Really? I'd love to," Veronica told her.

"Okay, be ready in an hour. I'll pick you up then," Laura said.

"I'll be ready, Laura," she said.

Veronica was finished getting dressed when she heard a car pull up. Laura came to the door.

"Right on time," Veronica said.

"I always try to be punctual," Laura told her.

"Yes, that's you, Laura," Veronica said.

Laura and Veronica talked about the job she would do.

"You can try announcing and see if you like it," Laura told her.

"I'm sure I will like it. At least I will have something to do," Veronica told her.

"Since Shelby is home, I'll help you," Laura said.

"Okay, thanks," she said.

They walked into the building, down the corridor, to Laura's office.

Veronica sat on the couch, and Laura at her desk. Then, Samuel came in.

"Hi, Veronica. It's me, Samuel," he said.

"Oh, hi, Samuel. I'm here to do some announcing," she told him.

"Yes, I heard. You'll do great," he told her.

"I hope so," she said.

"Go get the dolphins ready, Samuel. Then you can bring Ronnie in," Laura said.

"It should only be about a half hour," Laura told Veronica.

"That's fine," Veronica said.

Samuel came back.

"We are just about ready," he told them.

"Well, wish me luck, Laura," Veronica said.

Veronica took Samuel's arm, and he walked her to the podium, near the dolphin pool. Veronica could hear the crowd settling in on the benches. She was a little nervous.

It was time now. The lights were on the trainer and the dolphins. The microphone was on.

"Ladies and gentlemen, please welcome Wendy and Wally, with trainer Samuel," Veronica said, her voice strong.

The crowd loved the show and applauded.

Laura came to get Veronica, and they walked back to the office.

"You were fantastic," Laura told her.

"It was fun. I really liked announcing, I miss performing, but at least this is something for me to keep busy," Veronica said.

"Well, I am glad you are back, Ronnie," Laura told her.

"So am I," she said.

"So, are you up for one more show, Ronnie?" Laura asked.

I sure am," Veronica said.

"Then I'll bring you back," Laura told her.

After Veronica finished her second announcing show, Laura got ready to take her home.

Laura drove Veronica to the cottage and helped her inside. "You need anything before I go?" Laura asked.

"No, I'm fine. Thanks again for everything," Veronica said.

Laura drove off.

A short while later, Veronica heard another car. It was Tess. She came to the door and knocked.

"The door is open," Veronica said.

"Hi, Ronnie. How was the aquarium today?" Tess asked.

"It went well. I announced two shows," Veronica said.

"That's great. So, are you going to do that for work?" Tess asked.

"Yes, for a while," Veronica said.

"Well, I'll start dinner. Will you join me tonight?" Tess asked.

"Sure, if you like. I'm sorry about the other night. I guess I never know what I'm doing anymore," Veronica told her.

"No, I'm sorry. It was my fault," Tess said.

"Still friends?" Veronica said.

"Always friends," Tess told her.

"Great goes for me, too," Veronica said.

"Come to the house, and talk to me while I get dinner ready," Tess told her.

"Okay, I'll be there in a few minutes. Shelby and I should walk," Veronica said.

"Okay, take your time," Tess told her.

Veronica and Shelby walked for a while, then headed to the house. They walked into Tess' kitchen.

"Smells good again, Tess," Veronica said.

"Sit at the table. The food will be done soon," Tess said.

"So, Tess, I was wondering. You don't seem to go out much," Veronica said.

"Well, ever since my girlfriend and I broke up, I don't feel like it," she said.

"You must still miss her," Veronica said.

"Some days more than others," Tess told her.

"You must miss Trevor?" Tess asked.

"Some days I miss him, yes," she said.

"We just have to keep you moving forward," Tess told her.

"Yes, we do. If you ever need some company, I'm just next door," Veronica told her.

"You never know, I just might sometime," Tess said.

Tess and Veronica finished their dinner.

"That was real good chicken, Tess," Veronica told her.

"Would you like some more wine?" Tess asked Veronica.

"Yes, just one more please," she said.

Tess gave Veronica another glass of wine and sat with her.

"If you don't mind me saying, your girlfriend was crazy to let you go," Veronica said to Tess.

"I guess it takes two," Tess said.

"Yes, that is true," Veronica agreed.

The phone rang.

"It's your mom," Tess told her.

"Hello, Mom," Veronica said.

"Hi, dear. I tried to call your place, but no answer, so I figured you were with Tess," her mom said.

"Yes, we just finished dinner. I was just going back to the cottage," Veronica told her.

"Just wanted to talk to you about Melissa's graduation. It's in two weeks," her mom said.

"I know, Mom. I won't be able to make it, but I did send her something," Veronica said.

"Well, we hope you change your mind, Ronnie," her mom said. "If I do, I'll call you," she said.

Veronica hung up the phone.

"How is your mom doing?" Tess asked.

"She's good. She wants me to go to Melissa's graduation," Veronica said.

"You don't want to go?" Tess asked.

"Not really. You see I have this problem -- I can't see a thing," Veronica said jokingly.

Tess laughed.

"You are funny, Ronnie," Tess told her.

"Then be with me," Ronnie told her.

"What do you mean?" Tess asked.

"Let's try to be with each other. Give me a chance," Veronica said.

I'll think about it. I really do like you," Tess told her.

"Is it because I'm blind?"

"No, silly. Quit making me laugh," Tess said.

"I like it when you laugh," Veronica told her.

"All right, Ronnie, if you want, we can try," Tess told her.

"Really?" Veronica said.

Tess sat on the couch next to Veronica.

"You sure you want this?" Tess asked.

"Yes, I do want this," Veronica told her.

Tess leaned over and kissed Veronica softly on her mouth.

"Was that okay?" Tess asked.

"Yes, I like it. Your lips are so soft; makes me feel good inside," Veronica told her.

"I feel good inside when I am with you," Tess told her.

"Stay with me tonight, Ronnie, if you feel comfortable, with me," Tess told her.

"I'd love to stay with you tonight," Veronica said to her.

The next morning, a Saturday, Tess was up early.

Tess went into the bedroom where Veronica was.

"You awake, Ronnie?" Tess asked.

"Just waking up now," she said.

"Good morning," Tess said.

"Good morning, Tess. Did you sleep well?" Veronica asked.

"I sure did. How about you, Ronnie?" Tess asked.

"Yes, I did. Last night was wonderful with you, Tess," Veronica told her.

"I really enjoyed it, too," Tess told her.

"You working today, Tess?" Veronica asked.

"I have the whole day and night off," she said.

"I just have errands to do. Is Laura picking you up today?" Tess asked.

"She is supposed to by noon," Veronica said.

"I'll be back before then. Call her and tell her I'll bring you in today," Tess told her.

"You don't have to do that," Veronica said.

"I want to. Then we can spend time together," Tess said.

"Okay, great. I love our time together," Veronica told her.

Tess kissed Veronica good-bye, then was out the door.

Veronica was excited about her new relationship. She wasn't sure what it was, but she really liked it.

Veronica called the aquarium and left Laura a message about the ride. Then she and Shelby went for a walk.

The phone was ringing as Veronica and Shelby were walking back inside.

"Hello," she answered.

"Hi, Ronnie. It's me, Trevor.

"Hi, Trevor," she said.

"Are you busy today?" he asked.

"Well, actually Tess is taking me to do some work at the aquarium," she told him.

"You working again?" he asked.

"Yes, announcing the shows," she told him.

"Well, that's good," he said.

"It's better than sitting around," she told him.

"Do you mind if I stop by your work for a minute?" he asked.

"Sure, but I haven't changed my mind," she told him.

"I know," he said.

"Okay then, see you in a little while," she told him.

Tess came back, and they were on their way to the aquarium.

"You doing okay today, Ronnie? You seem quiet," Tess said.

"I'm fine, just thinking," she said.

"You aren't changing your mind about us, are you?" Tess asked her.

"No, I'm not changing my mind about us. Trevor called. He's coming to see me at the aquarium," she said.

"Does he want you back?" she asked.

"I don't know, but I told him I haven't changed my mind about him and me," she told Tess.

"Well, you decide what you want," Tess told her.

"I know what I want, Tess. I want you," Veronica said.

"Well, good, because I want to be with you, too," Tess told her.

Tess touched Veronica's shoulder.

Minutes later they pulled into the aquarium parking lot.

Tess kissed Veronica before they got out of the car.

"You don't mind if I stay and watch, do you, Ronnie?" Tess asked.

"No, I'd love you to stay," Veronica told her.

They walked inside and found Trevor there waiting.

They said their hellos.

"Just give me a few minutes, okay, Trevor?" Veronica said.

"Sure, take your time," he told her.

Tess walked Veronica to the lounge and helped her sit down.

"You sure you want to talk to him?" Tess asked.

"Yes, I want this over once and for all," Veronica said.

"I'll tell him to come in. I'll wait outside," Tess said.

Tess walked out to Trevor.

"She's all set if you want to go in," Tess told Trevor.

"Okay, thanks," he said.

Trevor walked into the room. Veronica said nothing.

"Ronnie, I've been thinking about us a lot," he told her.

"I have, too, Trevor," she said.

"What have you been thinking?" he asked.

"Just that I loved what we had, I still love you as a best friend, but I can't marry you or be with you," she told him.

"Well, you know I will always love you, Ronnie," he told her.

"I know, Trevor. You deserve someone who loves you deeper than I can," Veronica said.

"So, how are you and Tess getting along?" he asked.

"Very well actually. She's a great woman," Veronica said.

"I saw you and her earlier in the car. She kissed you," he said.

"Yes, she did. We are together. I really like her. She has helped me out a lot," Veronica told him.

"Well, I hope you are happy, Ronnie. If you ever need anything, just pick up the phone. Don't ever hesitate to call me," he told her.

"If I ever need you, I will call you, Trevor, I promise," she told him.

Veronica stood up, and Trevor walked over to her and gave her a big hug.

They both had tears in their eyes.

He kissed her and walked out the door.

As Tess was walking down the hall, she stopped Trevor.

"You okay?" she asked him.

"Yes, I am, Tess, Veronica told me about you and her." he said.

"She did? We really do care for each other," Tess told him.

"Take care of her. She really means a lot to me," he said sadly.

"I won't hurt her, I promise you that. You are a good man, Trevor," Tess told him.

"If she ever needs anything, I told her to call me," he said.

"She's very lucky to have you as a good friend," Tess told him.

Trevor touched her shoulder, then walked away.

Tess went back into the room and saw that Veronica was crying. Tess sat down beside her and held her.

"You okay, sweetie?" Tess asked.

"Yes, I'm glad you are here with me," Veronica said.

Tess gave Veronica a few tissues.

"Dry you eyes. You have to announce soon," Tess told her.

Just then Laura and Samuel came in.

"Hi, Ronnie, you okay?" Laura asked.

"Yes, I'm ready to announce," Veronica said.

"Samuel and I were talking. We know how you love to work with the dolphins, so I would like you and Samuel to do it together," Laura told her.

"How?" she asked.

"You ride in the boat. He will stay behind you and be your support, and you hold the hoops for the dolphins to jump," Laura said.

"I might be nervous at first," Veronica said.

"Let's try it. If you get nervous, you can just announce," Samuel said.

"Try it, Ronnie," Tess said.

"Sure, why not? What have I got to lose?" Veronica told Samuel.

Veronica went with Samuel to practice.

"You got a minute, Tess?" Laura said.

"Yes, sure," she said.

"You and Ronnie seem to be getting along great. She seems happy, even since her accident," Laura said.

"She's pretty amazing with all that has happened to her," Tess said.

"Well, I think it's great, you and her," Laura said.

"How did you know?" Tess asked.

"I know. I'm glad you both seem good together," Laura told her.

"Thanks, Laura. You are all right," Tess said.

"Let's go watch Samuel and Ronnie practice," Laura said.

Samuel and Veronica practiced for two hours, then took a break. Laura and Tess came over to them.

"You both look good out there. Do you want to try a show for tonight or tomorrow night?" Laura asked.

"Let's try tonight," Veronica said.

"I agree," Samuel said.

"Okay, see you both out there in three hours. Make it good," Laura told them.

It was almost showtime.

While Veronica was waiting in the lounge with Tess, Laura came in.

"You sure you're up for this challenge, Veronica?" Laura asked.

"Yes, I am ready for anything," Veronica told her.

"Okay, you have fifteen minutes," Laura told her.

"Thanks, Laura, for everything," Veronica said.

"Anything for you, hon," she said.

Laura hugged her and went out front.

"You'll do great, Ronnie," Tess told her.

"I'm glad you are here with me, Tess," Veronica told her.

"Everyone is here to cheer you on, I called your family," Tess told her.

"Oh, great! Now the pressure is on," Veronica said, laughing.

"I just want you to know I really care about you, Ronnie," Tess said.

"I know you do. I feel the same way about you, Tess," Veronica told her.

"You better go. You are on. Knock 'em dead, baby," Tess said.

"I will with you watching," Veronica told her.

"Kiss me for good luck," Veronica said to Tess.

Tess kissed Veronica softly on her lips.

"Okay, go now. I have to get to work," Veronica told her.

The lights were on the water. "Ladies and gentlemen, welcome Veronica and Samuel," the announcer said.

The show got lots of applause and even a standing ovation. It was clearly a success.

Veronica's family was so proud. They all stood up with their hands in the air and shouted, "Way to go, Ronnie!"

THE END.

VERONICA'S
CHALLENGE
CONTINUES

"**T**his is the last box" Tess said to Veronica.

"Good, we can relax for a few minutes." Veronica said.

"I'm glad we bought this house," Veronica told Tess.

"Yes" Tess agreed.

"Let me make us some tea." Tess said.

"Sounds good to me." Veronica said.

"I am glad we are together." Veronica told Tess.

"Me too, Ronnie." Tess said.

"Do you want to order some Chinese food?" Tess asked.

"Sure, I could go for some Chinese food." Respond Veronica.

Before they knew, they were eating their fried rice and egg rolls.

"This was a good idea!" Veronica said to Tess.

"Where is Shelby" Tess asked.

"He is lying next to the door on the rug" Ronnie said.

"How about a glass of wine" Tess said to Veronica, Veronica nodded her head, yes. They both sat their sipping wine and finishing dinner.

"I thought we could kiss for a while," Tess murmured to Veronica as she bent over and gave Veronica a lengthy kiss.

"Yes," Veronica concurred.

Veronica took Tess' hand and led her into the bedroom while they were still kissing.

"I want to make love to you Ronnie," Veronica said as she sat down on the bed. Tess removed Ronnie's blouse and kissed her once more.

"Please remove my bra..." Tess, Ronnie said.

Tess kissed Ronnie's neck, then lowered her mouth down to her breast, sucking on Ronnie's left breast, and Ronnie said, "that feels so good..."

I am just getting started Tess told Ronnie. "You know just how to make me feel good, Tess," Ronnie said.

"I am just getting started, Ronnie." Tess kissed Ronnie three times as she slid her mouth down toward her tummy.

"Go lower, Ronnie" said to Tess.

"Oh, yes I am babe." Tess kissed Ronnie lower, that's the spot Veronica moaned a little.

"Taste me" Ronnie said to Tess.

"I am, you taste so good" Tess said to Ronnie. Veronica moaned a little louder.

"Oh my gosh, that is the best feeling in the world, I love you Tess, I love you to honey.

Veronica told Tess to lay on her back, she kissed her deeply, "I love your kisses Ronnie," Tess' said and moaned.

"I am going lower" Ronnie said. Ronnie kissed Tess's belly, then went lower.

"Ooh that feels so good," Tess said.

The phone was ringing. "oh geez," said Ronnie.

Tess answered the phone, "It's for you Ronnie."

"Hello" Ronnie said.

"Ronnie, this is mom, your dad is in the hospital,"

"What happened mom?"

"He had a heart attack. Oh no Veronica!" said with her voice stuttering.

"We will be right there, mom."

Veronica was shaking, "My dad had a heart attack, let's get to the hospital" she told Tess.

"Come on Shelby," Veronica and Tess said as they dressed and got into the car.